PAIR-IT BOOKS™

It Sounds Like Music

Written by Sarah Vazquez

STECK-VAUGHN
COMPANY

ELEMENTARY • SECONDARY • ADULT • LIBRARY

A flute can sound like a singing bird.

A trumpet can make a blast.

A saxophone can sound like a honking goose.

A violin can be played very fast.

A piano can sound like thunder and rain.

A drum can make a boom.

Put them together, and what do you hear?
A symphony in your room!